PEGASUS

INTEGRATING THEMES IN LITERATURE AND LANGUAGE

THE LITTLE RED HEN

Retold by
Kathryn A. Shaw

Illustrated by
Cathy Craig Elling

KENDALL HUNT PUBLISHING COMPANY
2460 Kerper Boulevard P.O. Box 539 Dubuque Iowa 52004-0539

Once upon a time, there was a little red hen.

She lived with a lazy cat,
a lazy pig,
and a lazy duck.

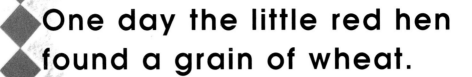

One day the little red hen found a grain of wheat.

4

"Who will help me plant the grain of wheat?" she asked.

"Not I," said the cat.
"Not I," said the pig.
"Not I," said the duck.
So she did it herself.

The wheat grew,
and grew,
and grew.

When the wheat was ripe
the little red hen asked,
"Who will help me cut
and thresh the wheat?"

"Not I," said the cat.
"Not I," said the pig.
"Not I," said the duck.
So she did it herself.

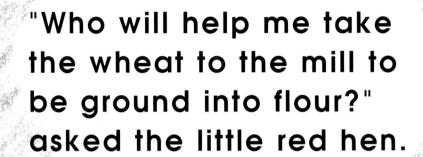

"Who will help me take the wheat to the mill to be ground into flour?" asked the little red hen.

"Not I," said the cat.
"Not I," said the pig.
"Not I," said the duck.
So she did it herself.

"Who will help me make the flour into bread?" asked the little red hen.

"Not I," said the cat.
"Not I," said the pig.
"Not I," said the duck.
So she did it herself.

"Mmm, who will help me eat the bread?" asked the little red hen.
"I will," said the cat.
"I will," said the pig.
"I will," said the duck.

"No you won't," said the little red hen.
And she ate it all by herself.

15

THE END

BREAD

Written by
Kathryn Shaw

Farmers use tractors to prepare the ground and plant the seeds.

A combine cuts and threshes the wheat.

Big trucks are loaded with the wheat.

These trucks take the wheat to grain elevators, where it is stored.

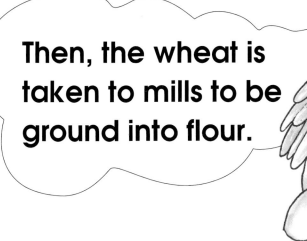

Then, the wheat is taken to mills to be ground into flour.

23

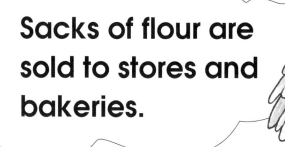

Sacks of flour are sold to stores and bakeries.

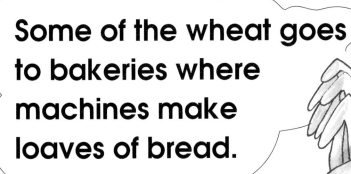

Some of the wheat goes to bakeries where machines make loaves of bread.

Trucks take
bread to stores.

People go to the store and buy bread...

...to share with friends.